TOO

BY SARA MADDEN

illustrated by hayley helsten

AuthorHouse™
1663 Liberty Drive
Bloomington, IN 47403
www.authorhouse.com
Phone: 1 (800) 839-8640

Published by AuthorHouse 05/17/2018

Library of Congress Control Number: 2018905042

ISBN: 978-1-5462-3940-6 (sc)
ISBN: 978-1-5462-3941-3 (e)

Print information available on the last page.

author**HOUSE**®

TOO

BY SARA MADDEN

illustrated by hayley helsten

For Tyler - Love, S.M. and H.H.

mine.

I LOVE YOU!

together♡

True Love

"Some families are created in *different ways* but are still, in *every way*, a family."
-Nia Vardalos

you're my favorite.

family

LOVE MY GIRLS!

forever ♡

5K RUN: LOVE IS

Joy is five years old. She has two dads named Tyler and Donnie. She also has two middle names, Shin and Mae. Joy and her two dads are on their way to Central Park for the festival.

Joy's best friend, Maya, is five years old, too.
Maya has two moms named Olivia and Ragi.

She has two last names, Smith and Goshai. Maya and her two moms are also headed to Central Park for the festival.

Joy and Maya meet by the pond where their parents have towed them in their wagons. They are each met by their two sets of grandparents, too.

Their first stop at the festival is the ice cream cart, where they order two cones with extra sprinkles.

The two scoops are too much for them to eat, so Joy's two dogs finish their cones.

Our Specialties ($1.00)
-watermelon berry swirl
-blackberry kiwi
-cotton candy
-strawberry lemonade sherbet
-vanilla with rainbow sprinkles

Later in the sandbox, Joy and Maya play with their friend Vee. He has one mom, one dad, and two sisters.

His parents kiss him on the cheek before sitting on the bench to watch him play just like Joy and Maya's parents did.

After playing in the sandbox, there's too much sand in their shoes to sit on the picnic blanket, so Joy and Maya empty them before they sit with their two dads and two moms.

Then, Joy and her two dads go to the field to fly
a kite with other familes while Maya and her two moms take
a walk over the bridge and back.

Their grandparents set up
the picnic, as always, with too much food.

After the picnic, their parents tow them in their two wagons around the park to see the different booths and entertainers.

At the carousel, Joy and Maya run into their friend Marco. Marco has one mom, one dad, one stepdad, and one baby sister.

They all enjoy the carousel ride together, with just a little too much laughter.

Marco and his family decide to join Joy and Maya at the swings. There, they see their friend, Sandy.

She has two dads, two moms, and two step brothers.
Everyone takes turns on the swings.

While Marco and Sandy stay at the swings with their families, Joy and Maya walk to the balloon cart. On their way, they see Tyler's friend, Tara, and her new baby.

After Joy and Maya get two balloons shaped like ducks, their parents tow them back to the stage to celebrate with their friends and family.

Joy and Maya take a quick nap. When they awake, they sit in front of the outdoor movie screen

Sandy, Marco, Vee, Tara, and their families are there, too.

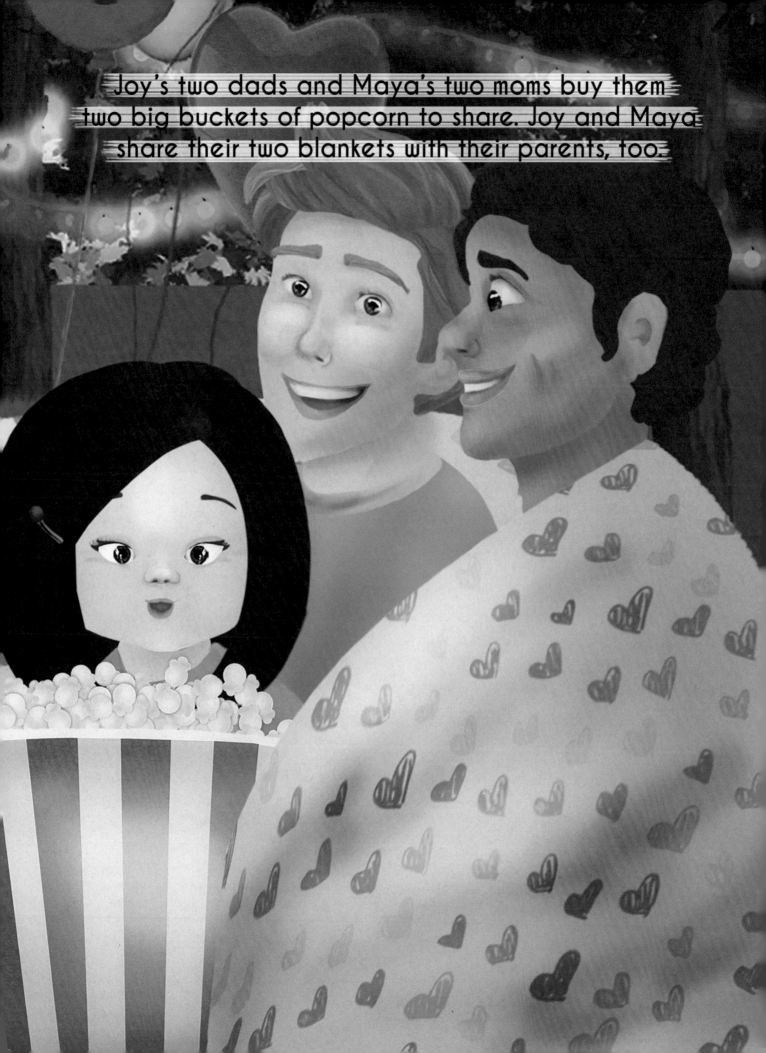

Joy's two dads and Maya's two moms buy them two big buckets of popcorn to share. Joy and Maya share their two blankets with their parents, too.

Joy, Maya, Marco, Sandy, and Vee all enjoy the evening with their friends and their different families.

There is so much laughter, too much popcorn, and lots of love.

Joy and Maya are happy that there is no such thing as too much love.

About the Author:

Sara Madden, who may or may not be a witch, grew up on California's Central Coast. She was raised on donuts and cookies provided by her grandparents' Tan Top Bakery. Her first story was written at age six, titled "I Love My Family," and she's been writing ever since.

Growing up dyslexic (and her continued fun with it into adulthood), Sara always has and always will find comfort in words, imagination, and believing in the unbelievable.

She currently lives in Utah with her adorable family, who may or not be completely bonkers. She has four unreliable guard dogs, eight clocks that refuse to tell time, and one unremarkable trampoline. Buttery popcorn and cinnamon cake donuts are her favorite food. And she never, ever, never, ever, never leaves home without a stick of vanilla or cake batter lip balm in her pocket (her taste's are undeniably fantastic!). In her spare time, she loves to paint and roller skate, but never at the same time-messes are dangerously unavoidable (she knows-she's tried it!).

Look for more of Sara Madden's books coming soon.
Follow Sara Madden and Tallulah Froom online:

SaraMaddenBooks.com
TallulahFroom.com

About the Illustrator:

Hayley grew up painfully shy but full of wonder. Her cheesy but adorable parents and seven crazy siblings brought her love and laughter, but she rarely spoke outside her home until she was a teenager. She did, however, find plenty of opportunities to express herself, dancing everywhere she went and drawing on every surface she could find. She fought every day to be happier, healthier, and weirder.

Hayley has grown (slightly) taller and wiser since those days, but she still believes life's greatest joys are dancing in public, laughing until you cry, and eating chocolate chip cookies for dinner.

She now gets to enjoy life with her cute husband Jeffrey and their happy baby Lucy. They live part time in their small but cute home in Utah, and part time in their VW bus named Magnolia. Both homes are full of kisses and covered in illustrations of all kinds.

Check out more of Hayley's work at HayleyHelsten.com!